The River Challenge

The River Challenge

Bear Grylls

Illustrated by Emma McCann

Bear
Grylls

First American Edition 2019
Kane Miller, A Division of EDC Publishing

First published in Great Britain in 2017 by Bear Grylls, an imprint
of Bonnier Zaffre, a Bonnier Publishing Company
Text and illustrations copyright © Bear Grylls Ventures, 2017
Illustrations by Emma McCann

For information contact:
Kane Miller, A Division of EDC Publishing
PO Box 470663
Tulsa, OK 74147-0663
www.kanemiller.com
www.edcpub.com
www.usbornebooksandmore.com

Library of Congress Control Number: 2018946314

Printed and bound in the United States of America
2 3 4 5 6 7 8 9 10

ISBN: 978-1-68464-096-6

To the young survivor
reading this book for the first time.
May your eyes always be wide open
to adventure, and your heart full
of courage and determination to
see your dreams through.

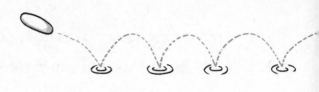

1

SHALLOW-END BOY

Jack stood a safe six feet away from the water, and turned the stone over in his fingers. It was light and flat.

"Okay," he said. "Here goes."

"You need to stand closer," his friend Joe interrupted.

Jack shook his head. "Here's fine, thanks."

The boys were on the gravel shore by the lake at camp. Out on the water a dinghy sailing lesson was going on.

Jack's stone was just the right size for him to wrap his thumb and first finger around. He drew his arm back, and flicked his wrist. The stone shot out of his fingers like a tiny Frisbee. Its spinning flat surface hit the water – and it bounced. The stone skipped across the lake away from Jack and he counted every splash it made before it finally sank.

"Nine! Record!" Jack shouted happily.

"Fluke," Joe said with an easy grin. He looked over at their friend. "Hey, you going to join in, Charlie?"

"Mmph."

Charlie was Joe's tentmate. He was sulking with his hands in his pockets. Jack and Joe both knew he would rather be guiding a space fighter through a field of asteroids than skipping stones. Unfortunately for Charlie, his tablet was charging in the leaders' office, where it had to stay during activity time.

Joe and Jack rolled their eyes at each other.

"Okay, my turn," Joe said. "Stand by for excellence."

Joe carefully wrapped his fingers around his stone, poised, and threw.

"… seven … eight … nine … TEN!" Joe grinned with delight. "Think you can top that?"

"No probs," Jack replied.

But Jack knew that it would take some beating. He needed to find the perfect stone. He wanted the flattest, roundest stone he could find. But he carefully

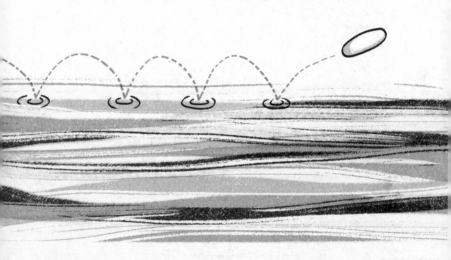

stayed near the top of the beach as he searched, and tried not to make it look like he was avoiding the water.

So Jack didn't notice Joe sidle over to Charlie and murmur something in his ear. Joe and Charlie strolled casually down the beach until they were standing on either side of Jack.

Then Joe grinned and looked sideways at Charlie. "Get him!"

Charlie and Joe grabbed Jack's arms and started to haul him toward the water.

"Hey, no! Cut it out! *Cut it out!*" Jack yelled. He dug his feet in and tried to pull back. "Get off! Get off me!"

The other two only pulled harder.

"Come on, Jack!" Charlie shouted happily. "Dunking time!"

"No! *No!*" Jack screamed. "*Get off!*"

He could feel panic rising as he struggled. The water was right ahead, waiting to swallow him up.

"Hey! Boys!" One of the sailing instructors shouted across from the lake. "Knock it off!"

Joe and Charlie slackened off a bit. Jack pulled himself free immediately and ran back up the beach until he was a safe distance from the water.

"What were you doing?" he yelled.

The other boys stared at him. The smiles on their faces were fading as they realized how upset he was.

"Gee, sorry," Joe mumbled. "It was just a joke. You know, just to get your feet wet."

"What's the big deal?" Charlie asked. "You can swim, can't you?"

"Of course I can swim!" Jack shouted.

"So what's the problem?"

"The problem ... the problem is ..." Jack spluttered.

He knew what the problem was. He just couldn't put it into words because he knew how silly it would sound if he did.

Jack hated water.

He could swim – from one side of the shallow end to the other. But he had never gone any farther because he couldn't stand up in the deep end, so he'd always managed to find excuses to miss swimming lessons.

Jack gave up trying to explain.

"We were playing a good game," he complained. "Why did you have to go and spoil it?"

"I'm sorry," Charlie said sincerely.

"I didn't know you'd mind," Joe added.

"Yeah, well, just leave it, okay," Jack muttered. "See you later."

Jack knew he would forgive them. They were his friends and he could tell they hadn't meant to hurt him. It had just been a joke.

But right now he was embarrassed and felt silly. He didn't want to be with them, or anywhere near the water, so he walked away.

2

CONTROL POINT

Jack jogged through the woods, with a map in one hand and a compass in the other. Joe ran alongside him, happy to let Jack do the map reading. Charlie was with them too, lagging a bit behind. They were friends again.

Jack's embarrassment yesterday hadn't lasted long. He'd helped a girl called Chloe rescue a chick that had fallen out of its nest by the lake. Chloe had been given a wildlife welfare badge, and Jack had made a new friend. And Chloe had given him something to say "thank you" – a compass.

Then Jack had made up with the boys over dinner in the evening. Joe and Charlie had let Jack have some of their chips and they had agreed that Jack could choose the first activity for the next day. Jack had chosen orienteering.

Players were given a compass and a flimsy, clear plastic wallet containing a map and a clue sheet. The sheet was marked with directions and symbols of things that players had to look for, like tracks or hills. Players had to find their way through the woods between control points. Everyone got a slightly different route to follow, so that no one could just follow another group. Every control point had a special stamp to mark your sheet, to prove you had been there. Jack was enjoying himself. He liked the way it tested his mind and his body at the same time. Joe was getting into it too, though he couldn't read a map at all. Charlie couldn't see why you didn't just use a map app instead of bothering with a compass and the clues.

The boys had done three control points so far. At first, Charlie had claimed the compass, but after a couple of times when he'd forgotten that the needle pointed two ways, and sent them in exactly the wrong direction, Jack used the compass Chloe had given him.

"Next control point should be dead ahead ..." Jack said as he checked the compass.

They came to a clearing in the trees, which had a ditch with a wooden plank across it. Across the clearing there was a small cliff, and the dark opening of a cave. A girl called Fatima was hanging around outside it.

"That must be it," Jack said. He had to hold the map wallet in both hands because it was so flimsy. He tried to hold

the map and the compass together so he
could check the direction, but something
was wrong. The dial was just spinning
around, and for a moment it looked like
there were five directions on it.

"Hey, Charlie – can you help check
the direction?" Jack asked. "This thing's
busted."

Charlie checked the official compass.

"Yup. We're going the right way," he reported. "This must be it."

Jack called over to Fatima. "Is this the control point?"

"In the cave," she called back.

"Cool," said Joe. "Let's go."

He and Charlie ran across the plank. Jack started – and immediately stopped.

The plank went over a stream.

Jack's feet skidded to a halt as if they had a mind of their own. They *did not* want to cross that stream. Nor did the rest of him. He knew it was silly. The stream wouldn't even come up to his knees. But when Jack tried to take a step forward his legs were wobbling.

"Oh, come on!" he muttered to himself. "I can do this!"

Whenever he felt the fear start to grip him, Jack thought of his swim across the pool. He had done it, even though it had been the scariest experience of his life. But he hadn't been back in the water since, and his fear had gotten worse and worse every year.

It was always the same. First his legs started wobbling. Then his stomach too. Then he started to feel short of breath.

Charlie and Joe hadn't noticed anything yet. But Jack knew that in a couple of seconds they would realize he wasn't there. They would look around.

If Jack didn't want them to find out about his fear, that was how long he had to get across – a couple of seconds.

Jack forced his foot forward again onto the plank. Then he moved his other foot past it.

Now his stomach was wobbling.

And so was the plank.

And then so was Jack.

"Aargh!"

He flung his arms out on either side. In his panic, his sense of balance just left him.

Jack waved his arms and wiggled his hips, trying to get his balance back. The clearing, the plank, the stream – they were all swimming around him.

He made himself break into a run for the last bit.

But somehow his foot missed the plank altogether and he plunged headfirst into the stream.

The fall seemed to take forever. Jack could see the stream coming up to meet him. The water was clear and he could see the pebbles on the bottom. Jack yelled and flung his arms out to break his fall.

But his hands didn't hit the bottom. He just kept going. *Splash!* Jack felt the water close over him and he just kept going down, deeper and deeper.

Finally, at last, he hit the bottom. His heartbeat pounded in his ears, and his lungs were bursting. He pushed with his feet and kicked as hard as he could upward.

3

RIVER WILD

Jack's head broke the surface. Water streamed down his face and blinded him. He scrabbled to clear it, spluttering and heaving.

"Over here," a man's voice called. Jack churned the water as he splashed blindly around. He had the horrible feeling that any moment now the water would swallow him altogether.

At last he felt someone take his hand and pull him out of the water.

Jack wiped the drops from his eyes.

A tanned, dark-haired man smiled down at him.

"You made quite a splash," the man said, smiling.

Now that Jack was on dry land his heart began to slow down to its normal speed. He was so embarrassed. It was bad enough that Joe, Charlie and Fatima had seen him fall, but to be rescued by a leader was too much. He tried to laugh it off while he looked around for his friends.

"I guess I did."

But his friends weren't there.

Nor was the clearing.

Nor were the woods.

Jack turned a slow circle to take in what he *could* see, with his eyes wide and his mouth hanging open.

Mighty walls of rock towered above him on either side. They had to be hundreds of feet high. He was standing at the bottom of a deep gorge.

A deep river gorge. A torrent of gray-brown water zipped past his astonished eyes. Its surface tossed and turned like a wild animal.

The banks were lined with rocks. The man had pulled Jack out of a shallow pool where the water swirled like a lazy whirlpool.

Beyond the rocks was a thin strip of forest. Jack could see trees and what looked like bamboo.

He recognized it from his local nursery, though these stalks were greener, more knobbly and way, way bigger. And beyond the forest were the cliffs.

Without realizing it, he hugged himself and shivered. A cold wind was blowing down the gorge and it cut right through his wet clothes.

"We can do introductions later," the man said with a smile, "but the first thing is to change out of that wet gear. I've got just the thing."

The man rummaged through his backpack and pulled out a sweatshirt, a dry pair of pants, and a waterproof jacket, together with some woolly socks.

Jack ducked behind a rock to get changed. He could worry about where he was later. Right now he was cold and wet, and he needed to fix that.

He felt like a new boy in his dry clothes. The feeling started at his feet as he pulled on the warm, soft socks, and worked its way up.

"Better?" the man asked with a laugh as Jack walked back around the rock. "You just can't beat the feeling of putting cold, wet feet into something dry. You'd better put these on, too. Where we're going the ground's going to be uneven and slippery, so you'll need more grip and support than sneakers can give you."

He set a pair of hiking boots on the rock, and held out his hand.

"I'm Bear, and I'm going to help guide you out of here."

Jack shook his hand.

"Thanks. I'm Jack." He didn't really know what else to say.

Jack sat down so he could pull the boots on. And then a horrible thought struck him as he looked at the water. *How* exactly would they get out of here?

"To get out … we're not going *on* the river, are we …?" Jack asked.

Bear shook his head with a smile.

"Not while it's in that mood. Take a look."

Jack looked. The surface of the river was churning. A submerged tree trunk broke through like a submarine coming

up for air, and was swept away like it weighed nothing.

"Now that could really upset your day if it hit your raft," Bear said, as they watched the trunk disappear downstream. "There'll be all kinds of hidden debris that could sink us or pin us down underwater if it hit. There'll be currents and eddies that could trap us. No, for now, we're on foot."

Suits me! Jack thought.

Jack stood up and shifted his weight from foot to foot, testing the boots. His feet felt secure and steady.

He took another look around. He still had no idea how he had gotten here, or how to get back to his friends at camp. But he wouldn't get anywhere by standing still and he could see that there was only one way out of the gorge. And if they were sticking to dry land, he'd be fine.

"Okay," he said. "I'm ready!"

Bear grinned.

"Let's do this, then."

They started to walk together along the rocky shore. The smooth round rocks turned and twisted under Jack's feet. The boots covered his ankles and supported his legs, and he was very grateful for their firm grip. Without that support, he would probably have twisted something.

After a couple of minutes the shore turned into a jumble of huge rocks. Some were the size of cars, and others were the size of houses. Jack and Bear climbed easily up onto the first one, then Bear walked a few paces across its flat three feet away, but there was a torrent of water rushing between them.

Bear turned to face Jack, with his hand held out.

"You okay?" he asked.

Jack still stared down at the water below.

No way was Jack getting over that gap. No way!

top to the far edge.

"Bit of a gap here …" Bear remarked. Without a pause, he stuck out one long leg and half jumped across the gap. "… but not that wide. I can give you a hand over."

Jack stopped. The rock stuck out into the river. The next rock was less than

4

ONE SMALL STEP

"Jack?" Bear said again. Then he asked kindly, "Is it the height?"

Jack shook his head.

"The water?"

Jack nodded miserably.

Bear's voice was encouraging. "Okay, let's do this in stages." He tapped his head. "Everything starts in the mind. You can't do anything if you don't *believe* you can, so that's the first stage. Forget

the water, just think of the distance. You can step that far, right?"

"Yes," Jack agreed reluctantly. He supposed it would be easier than walking across that plank at camp.

So Jack stuck out a foot, Bear grabbed his hand, and suddenly he'd gotten across.

"Way to go!" Bear said. "Now, let's plan ahead. We're high up enough to take a look at where we are."

Jack could see the river snaking away into the distance. Bear pointed and sketched out in the air the route they were going to take.

"You see where the river bends? If we follow the rocks there, we'll just end up in the water. So we are going to head up onto that higher bit of bank to get around it. The secret is that you're always looking ahead, always planning your next move. Then, when you get there, there's nothing to worry about because you're already prepared for it in your head." He smiled at Jack. "We'll do this together."

After that, it did get easier.

They had to jump over water again at the edge of the next rock, but Jack saw it coming. Bear was right – in his mind he had already put himself over on the other side. By the time he got to the gap, Jack's whole body felt committed to it.

He was still pleased when the rocks got higher and farther away from the water, though. The river was roughing up into three-foot-high waves, like it was threatening him for spoiling its fun. He was very happy to get into the trees between the bottom of the cliff and the river. The leaves rustled in the wind and muffled the sound of the water.

Jack didn't know much about trees, but he recognized some evergreens with pinecones and dark-green needles, like the ones back home. Other types he didn't know. And there were clumps of bamboo everywhere, its tall thin shafts wrapped in green leaves.

"We need to eat on the move if we're going to make progress," said Bear. "Are you hungry?"

"Um – yes, a little, I guess," Jack agreed. Bear took his backpack off, and Jack assumed he had some energy bars or cookies in there.

So he was quite surprised when Bear pulled out a serious-looking machete, with a blade as long as the distance between Bear's elbow and wrist. Bear went over to the nearest tree and chopped a couple of pinecones from a branch.

"Most parts of a pine tree are edible," Bear said. "Pine nuts are great energy, once you get them out of the cones. And you can make a decent tea out of pine needles. Full of vitamins A and C." He chopped both of the pinecones in two and started picking the small nuts out of the center of one. He passed the other cone to Jack. "Try it!"

Well, it wasn't quite the cookies Jack

had been expecting. He took the cone carefully and started to pry the little nuts out, then nibbled on them. They tasted ... well, pretty good, in fact.

Jack kept on nibbling as they walked.

Soon after that, Bear found a bush full of red berries shaped like little eggs.

"Goji berries – a great find," Bear said. He cut off a sprig for Jack and another for himself. "Cost a lot in your local supermarket, but grow here absolutely free. I think we can afford to take a quick break."

The two of them settled down on the ground, which was covered in a soft carpet of leaves and pine needles. Jack sat with his back to a cluster of bamboo.

"Are we going to eat this too?" he asked with a smile. "We seem to be eating everything else."

Bear laughed.

"Bamboo shoots are good if you boil them, but we won't be doing that on the move. The rest is just indigestible to humans. Here, drink this. We need to keep ourselves hydrated."

Bear took out a large canteen of water, and both he and Jack took long drinks.

"At least there's no danger of running out of this," Jack said, thinking of the river.

Bear nodded.

"True –" He stopped suddenly, with his head cocked. "Do you hear that?"

Jack listened. He could hear the wind in the trees, and the river in the distance, and birdsong, and …

And a kind of huffing, puffing, grunting noise. It wasn't a bird and it wasn't the wind or the water …

"An animal?" Jack asked quietly.

Bear nodded slowly.

"Definitely."

Jack didn't know what kinds of animals you got around here – but he knew that one making a noise like that must be big.

"Is it safe?" he whispered.

Bear slowly got to his feet. His face was thoughtful.

"Well, if it's what I think it is, we're going to have to tread very carefully," he murmured.

Jack braced himself. Would they have to make a run for it?

But Bear jerked his head toward the noise.

"And as long as we tread carefully, there's no reason not to go and see it," he said with a wry smile. "Come on. Follow me."

5

BEASTLY ENCOUNTER

Jack stuck close behind Bear as he followed the sounds. Bear seemed to know what he was doing, but Jack knew wild animals could be dangerous …

The grunting came from the other side of a thick cluster of bamboo. Jack could also hear a crunching noise. And there was a definite unwashed-animal smell. It smelled filthy and stinky yet also clean and healthy, all at the same time.

Bear peered through the bamboo stalks, then gently moved a couple to make a gap.

"Take a look," he murmured quietly.

Agog with curiosity, but still nervous, Jack looked.

"Oh … *wow!*" he whispered.

It was a panda. A real, live giant panda. At first, Jack thought it looked like a big black-and-white teddy bear, cute and cuddly like in all the pictures. It sat with its back legs stuck out in front of it. Its front claws held on to a thick stalk of bamboo, which it chewed with powerful jaws, *crunch, crunch, crunch.*

Then Jack looked closer, and he realized it wasn't cute and cuddly at all.

It was BIG. Sitting down, the panda was as tall as Jack. If it stood up on its back legs it would tower over him. Its black-and-white fur bulged with muscles under its skin. Jack reckoned it could pull him apart, if it wanted to. The claws that gripped the bamboo were as long as Jack's fingers, and about a thousand times sharper. And those teeth …

The bamboo stalk the panda was eating was about as thick as Jack's arm. He wouldn't be able to bend it even if he used all his strength. But the panda's jaws were strong enough to crunch through it like it was made of toffee.

The panda turned its head slowly and peered over at the two humans. Its jaws didn't miss a beat. *Crunch, crunch, crunch.* Then it slowly looked away again.

This wasn't a fluffy teddy bear. This was a wild creature living where it belonged. Jack and Bear were the strangers here. Jack felt like he had been allowed into someone's home – maybe a friend with strict parents. He could stay if he behaved himself and didn't do anything silly.

"We're super lucky to see this, Jack," Bear said quietly.

"I know!" Jack breathed. He couldn't take his eyes off it. "I didn't know there were many pandas still around nowadays."

"There aren't. Giant pandas still living wild – in the whole world, I reckon there are only a couple of thousand. If it wasn't for humans looking out for them, pandas would have become extinct years ago."

"Wow."

Bear smiled.

"Believe it or not, it's getting better. Just a couple of years ago, giant pandas stopped being officially 'endangered.' Now they're just 'vulnerable.' It's a small step, but it's a start."

Jack stared harder at the panda. He knew he would never get a chance like this again.

"I hope they make it," he whispered.

"Me too." Bear paused, then chucked slightly. "But you've got to feel sorry for them. They're meant to be meat eaters, but all they know how to eat is bamboo, which is terrible for nutrition. It's almost pure cellulose – that's the thing that makes plants rigid and chewy – and it's indigestible, like I said before. Pandas can only digest the tiny bit of bamboo that isn't cellulose, so to get enough energy, they can do little else *but* eat bamboo all day long to survive."

"So they're not dangerous?" Jack asked.

"Oh, they can be! Any animal can be dangerous if you provoke it, especially a wild one. A panda is a giant bear, after all. You've seen those claws and those teeth. If this was a mother and we got between her and her cub, we'd be in trouble. Even if you just tried to take its bamboo away, you'd probably lose an arm," Bear said. "That's why we're not getting any closer than this."

The panda agreed that they weren't getting any closer. Maybe it didn't like being stared at. It suddenly rolled forward to stand on all fours, and strolled away from them. As it pushed its way through the bamboo, its powerful body shoved the stalks aside like they were curtains.

The panda took a final look back at Jack and Bear, and spat out the chewed bamboo sticking out of its mouth. Then it disappeared into the undergrowth.

Jack realized he had been holding his breath. He let it out with a puff.

"Well," said Bear. "That was unexpected."

"It was amazing!" said Jack. He walked forward and picked up the piece of bamboo the panda had spat out. The end of it had been chewed

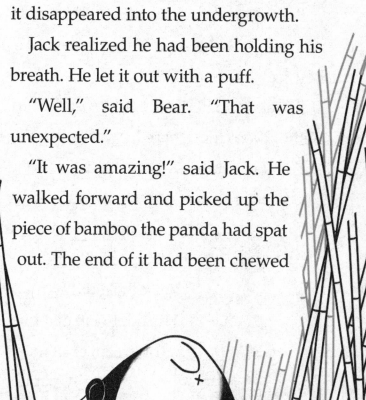

into stringy pieces. Jack slipped it into his pocket with a grin.

"Souvenir," he said.

Bear laughed. "You bet. This was worth remembering. Let's press on … hey, Jack, *watch out!*"

It was too late. Jack had taken a step without looking where he was going.

His foot plunged into something soft. The most revolting smell in the world rose up and hit him in the face.

Jack looked down.

His boot was in a pile of green, extremely smelly panda poop.

"YUCK!" Jack shouted.

He yanked his foot out of the pile in disgust. But as he stumbled backward, he sat down right in the middle of an even larger pile of dung.

Bear was trying not to laugh.

"Consider that another souvenir!"

6

EATING OUT

Jack's pants were damp from scrubbing, and he tried to ignore the smell.

Bear lay beside a pool on a rocky ledge beside the river, and carefully lowered his hands into the water as Jack watched.

"Slow and gentle," he said quietly. "We don't want to spook them."

There were two fish in the pool. The river had obviously once risen higher than the ledge, and this pool and the fish had been left behind when the water level had receded.

Bear lay completely still for a minute or more without moving his hands.

"Fish are sensitive to temperature changes, so my hands have to cool down to water temperature first. To stop them seeing my hand, I'm moving in slowly from behind the fish ..."

Bear suddenly flicked his hands out in a spray of water, and a wriggling, silver shape half as long as his forearm flew out and onto the bank. He pinned the fish down and, with his other hand, Bear hit the fish hard on the head with the handle of his machete.

"The other fella's gone over to your side, Jack," he said.

"Can you try to get that one?"

Jack stared at him. Bear knew how he felt about water.

Jack had managed to rinse his pants out in a stream because the water only came up to his knees and *anything* was better than smelling of panda poop.

But this was different. He'd need to get his face really close to the water, like Bear had done. He hated water on his face.

Then Jack remembered Bear's advice to do it in stages. First: believe you can.

And he could. Bear hadn't done anything that would exactly drown him.

"Yeah," Jack said. "Okay."

"You can do it, champ," Bear whispered.

So, Jack crawled forward and hung

his head over the side of the pool. He clenched his jaw as he glared at the water, inches from his face. He told himself that because he was already lying down, he wasn't going to fall in. Slowly, he lowered his hands in.

"Remember, give your hands a little time to cool down," Bear said.

So Jack lay there, with his hands in

the water and his breath catching in his throat.

"Okay. So ease your arm toward the back of the fish, and slowly slide under it," Bear whispered. "Then when you are as close to it as you can be, bring your hand up superfast and flick the fish onto the bank!"

Jack did as he was told and he could feel his arm shaking – half from the cold and half from the anticipation.

Jack's hands felt like blocks of ice and he was tempted just to try to grab the fish. But he held his nerve until his hand was underneath the fish.

The fish was now near the surface and close to the bank.

"Try it now," Bear said quietly.

With a burst of movement, Jack

whipped his hand up, fingers splayed wide to give him the best chance of catching the fish.

And there it was! A fish, flying through the air. It hit the rock and quick as a flash, Bear grabbed it and stunned it with his machete.

"Yes!" Bear said. "Well done."

Jack high-fived Bear. He was puffing with delight.

"Great job, Jack. Patient, brave, determined. I love it!" Bear looked straight at the boy. "Yep. Really great job! That's not easy to do."

"I know," Jack replied. "Especially as I don't really like water." He added quickly, "But I got it."

"That's why it's so impressive. You had to conquer some fears as well as hold your nerve. That takes courage."

As he spoke, Bear turned the machete around in his hand and sliced carefully along the belly of the first fish from head to tail.

"First thing you do with anything you catch is get the guts out," Bear said. He hooked his finger inside the fish's belly and pulled out a mass of slimy tubes. "They're the first thing that will go bad."

He did the same to the second fish, and chucked all the guts into the river.

"We'll make a fire to cook these," Bear said, "but first we need somewhere to camp for the night. Come on."

Catching the fish had taken longer

than Jack had realized. The tops of the cliffs were turning red with the setting sun as they headed back toward the woods.

Bear picked out a spot of flat ground between two pine trees about six feet apart. He got Jack to sweep it clean of leaves with a branch, while he selected a large cluster of bamboo.

"This stuff is like nature's scaffolding," Bear said. "You can use it to make anything you like."

He slashed through the base of a thick stalk with the machete.

"But for now we're just going to make a simple lean-to shelter, which is about the easiest kind there is," he said. "We're going to need vine to tie the poles together. Grab as much as you can; it should be about as thick as your finger."

Jack found vine growing everywhere, in strands several feet long. It wrapped around the trees, and covered the ground, and grew in thick layers over the walls of the gorge. It didn't take him long to gather what they needed.

Bear used some of Jack's vine to tie a bamboo pole horizontally between the two trees at shoulder height. Then he tied the top ends of more poles to the horizontal one and rested the bottom ends on the ground, until he had a whole row of sloping poles. He started to tie more horizontal poles along them.

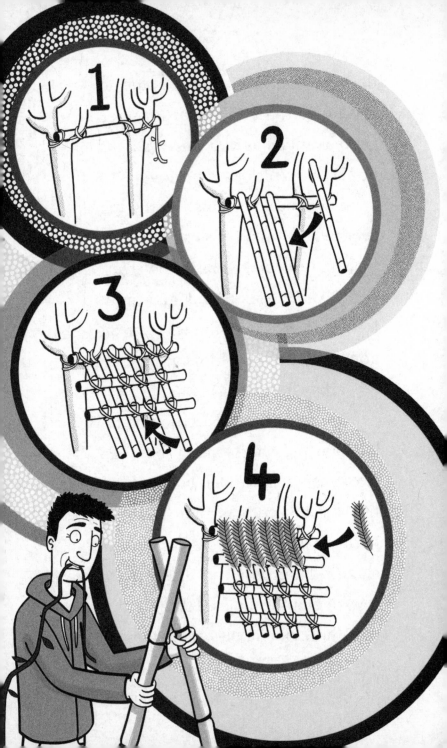

Bear was making a bamboo grid.

"We're going to need leafy branches to plug the gaps ..." he said as he worked.

So Jack took the machete and got busy on the trees and bushes around them, lopping off small branches with plenty of leaves so that Bear could weave them into the grid.

Soon the shelter had a thick layer of bushy branches on the top.

"Good work, Jack," Bear commented. "Let's add some more branches on the ground as well, to keep us warm from below, and then we'll be good for the night."

In what seemed like no time they had made themselves a shelter! It faced away from the wind, and its sloping roof trapped the heat of the fire that Bear then built in front of it.

The survival duo had a meal of cooked fish and pine-needle tea, which Bear boiled up with river water in a metal mug from his backpack.

After a long day, Jack could feel his eyes grow heavy and he thought it would be a good idea to lie down. But a moment later he was wide-awake again as Bear dumped a load of leaves and branches over him.

"Hey!"

"Keeps you warm," Bear said with a wink. "They trap a layer of air against you that your body can warm up. Sleep tight."

Jack was about to protest that he was perfectly warm without half a tree on

top of him, but his eyes were heavy again and he thought he would rest them just for a moment.

He woke up the next morning to the smell of fresh fish cooking, and felt more relaxed than if he had slept in the tent back at camp.

Then Bear looked up from the fire. He smiled, but somehow Jack sensed it was a nice way for Bear to deliver bad news.

"Morning, Jack," Bear said. "You okay?"

"I thought all this was a dream and I would wake up back at camp." He paused. "I guess not."

"You'll make it back. But first we have some work to do."

Bear sipped his tea and then passed a mug across to Jack.

"So, while you were sleeping, I had a look along the gorge. We've got a choice coming up. The good news is that the river's a lot slower and calmer than it was. The bad news is that about half a mile from here the shore disappears. No more walking space. The sides of the gorge come right down to the water."

Jack's face dropped. His heart began to thud.

"So," Bear said. "We can choose to be *in* the water, or we can choose to be *on* it."

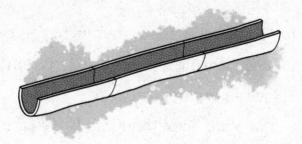

7

BAMBOO BUILDING BLOCKS

"That's our raft," Bear said a couple of hours later. "It just doesn't know it yet."

Jack and Bear were looking at two rectangles lying side by side on the ground. Each rectangle was made from bamboo, measured about three feet wide, with eight or nine poles in it, and about nine feet long.

Bear had cut down the thickest poles they could find: he had wrapped his hands around them and if his fingers touched, then the poles were too thin.

Jack stared in horror.

That's all? Jack thought. *That's all that will be between us and the water?*

Bear saw his face. "Remember ..." he began.

"I know," Jack said reluctantly. "Stage one: believe."

Okay, he believed bamboo could float.

"And stage two," Bear said, "is prepare. That's what we're doing now."

"Why are there two layers?" Jack asked, trying to force himself to concentrate on the plan.

"The poles of the top layer will fit into the gaps between the poles of the bottom one," Bear told him, "and together they'll keep it rigid enough for a man and a boy to sit on." He paused. "Two layers means we will be much more buoyant. That's going to be good for us in this river." Bear tapped the knobbly ridges that lined the poles. "Bamboo has natural watertight compartments, so it floats very easily. Right, let's measure it."

They both sat on the top layer. It wasn't quite wide enough for Bear's liking, so he added a few more poles.

"The raft's going to be top-heavy with us on it," he said. "The wider it is, the more stable it will be. Okay, now you need to untangle all that vine ..."

And so they got on to stage three: build it. Bear started to cut holes through each pole with his machete. One end, the other end, and in the middle.

Jack watched anxiously.

"Won't that let the water in?"

"It's watertight enough," Bear said. "Water will get in through these holes, but that's only three compartments per pole. There's plenty more that will stay dry."

Then came the trickiest part, and it

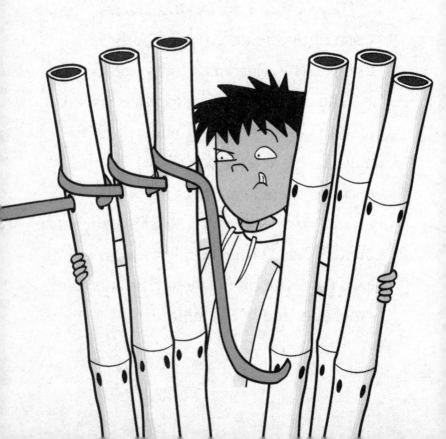

was a two-person job. Jack had to hold the bamboo together so that the holes all lined up, while Bear fed lengths of vine through them. He threaded it through the two holes of each pole, then wrapped it tight around the pole before he poked it through the next one.

Bear talked as he worked.

"Something I need to say, Jack. The river's smoother than it was, but there's no reason it can't get rough again. A survivor has to be prepared for anything and that includes, perhaps, even one of us ending up in the water."

He looked sideways at Jack.

"So we need to prepare ourselves for that, yes?" he asked. "Just in case. Forewarned is forearmed, remember."

Jack swallowed hard.

"Forewarned is ... what?" he said anxiously.

Bear smiled as he carefully pushed some vine through two more holes.

"Forewarned means we prepare ourselves that we might have to face some difficult things ahead. Forearmed means we equip ourselves with what we need to survive those difficulties. In this case, I need to show you what to do if you end up in the white water. You with me?"

Jack swallowed nervously. "Okay. I'm listening."

"First up, forget about any idea of swimming for safety."

"Really?" Jack asked in surprise.

"Really. You'll just wear yourself out. No one can fight a fast-flowing river. You will need to float, with attitude. Focused and determined. Got it?"

"Got it," Jack replied, although he wasn't quite sure he believed himself yet.

Bear continued. "Keep calm and keep floating until you're through the rapids and can spot a place where you can safely get to the shore."

"But how do I keep floating if it's crazy white water?"

"Get onto your back and go feetfirst. Your legs can take the impact if you hit anything, your head is protected and it's out of the water so you can see properly.

Your arms work calmly to keep you buoyant. After that, it's a bit like when we were walking. You just have to be always looking ahead, ready to make any quick decisions."

"Head out of the water, okay," Jack mumbled to himself.

"Steer yourself clear of any whirlpools or rocks up ahead," Bear went on. "Stick to the sides as much as you can, where it's slower and shallower. Unless you're going over a drop, maybe over a waterfall or through some rapids – then you steer for the *center* of the flow. It means you'll land in the deepest part, and you're away from anything that might bust you up."

Jack let the instructions swirl around in his head and settle down.

"I think I've got it …"

"And the last thing to remember is that when you're underwater, keep calm and gently swim for the surface. It's easy to get confused about which way is up, so follow the bubbles. They always know."

Jack was blinking back rising panic just hearing all these words.

Bear smiled at him.

"It's all going to be fine. We simply plan for the worst, prepare ourselves with the right skills and attitudes, and then we know that we can overcome anything the river can throw at us. It is simply about being prepared." He paused. "We will be good. Trust yourself."

Not quite sure, Jack smiled back.

Bit by bit, the loose collection of poles had turned into a raft while Bear was talking. Bear had also made them each a paddle from one pole of bamboo, cut in half and split down the middle.

They had a final snack of berries and pine nuts, and drank some water.

Then Bear tied one end of a length of vine to the raft, and held on to the other end.

Jack's heart started to pound behind his ribs. He knew what was coming.

"And now we launch," Bear said with a friendly smile.

Jack couldn't quite speak, but he nodded, and they each picked up a side of the raft.

The bamboo was hollow and light, so it all weighed a lot less than it looked,

but it was still big and Jack had to put all his strength into lifting it. Together, Jack and Bear carried the raft down to the river's edge to slide it in. It bobbed on the surface and Bear pulled it back so that it touched the shore.

"After you?" said Bear, indicating with his hand. He smiled when Jack hesitated. "Jack, to be a little scared is healthy; it's called respect. I feel it often too. It's our survival instinct reminding us to be smart and get it right. I know you can do this. You've got that survival spirit racing through you." He paused. "After all, you're the boy who helped to build this raft. Come on, we can do this."

Jack nodded silently, and braced himself.

You can do this, he muttered to himself.

So Jack crouched down and lowered himself onto the bamboo.

"Good lad, Jack. Now, nice and steady. Don't try to stand or it'll tip over," Bear advised. "Just crawl onto it, and shift down to the front end."

The raft sank a little under Jack's weight, and water splashed up between the poles. His body froze, every muscle locked in place.

But then Jack took a deep breath and made his muscles unlock.

"Don't worry about the water, Jack. It's there to help us get downstream. We are going to use it, not fear it."

Jack nodded and blinked.

"I can do this," he said under his breath.

The raft rocked as Bear climbed on behind him. More water sloshed through the poles, soaking Jack's knees and legs.

"Ready?" Bear asked.

"Ready," Jack whispered. "Let's just do it."

And with that, Bear used his bamboo paddle to push the raft out into the current.

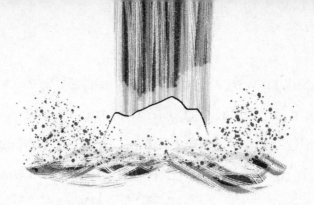

8

RIDING THE RIVER

Jack flinched as water washed over his knees.

"You know you've got the most important job?" Bear said behind him.

"Navigator?" Jack guessed.

Bear shook his head and laughed.

"Lookout! We can only go one way down the river, but we need to know what's coming. We need to keep to the slow water at the sides as much as we can, so we can get out of danger if we see big rapids ahead. But that means there's also more chance of us bumping over things, like submerged rocks, sunken trees …"

"Okay." Jack scanned the river ahead, looking for dangers. "But, wouldn't it help if you were at the front?"

"You're lighter than me," Bear explained. "If I was at the front then my weight would be less likely to ride over stuff. But it means we're relying on you."

"I'll do my best," Jack promised nervously.

Jack slowly moved his eyes from side to side across the river ahead. He saw the first obstacle almost immediately. There was a wave in the water up ahead, and it didn't move.

The raft was heading straight for a rock just under the surface that could smash it to pieces.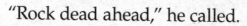

"Rock dead ahead," he called.

"Got it," Bear said. "Paddle left, and hard!"

They paddled the raft and it swept past the rock easily.

"Good work, Jack!"

The pair kept floating downstream, Jack scanning for obstacles and Bear giving instructions which way to paddle to keep the raft safe yet within striking distance of the shore.

Soon though, Jack spotted the next danger. A tree had its roots in a crack in the vertical cliff, but the rest of it had fallen into the water. The water

rippled and churned across its branches. "Tree up ahead," he called. "By the right cliff."

Jack and Bear paddled away from the slow water to get around it.

The raft began to rock and tremble as the fast, choppy water in the central channel moved underneath it and splashed up through the poles. Jack had to fight his fears not to shut his eyes and give up. He forced himself to keep his eyes open. Bear was depending on him.

Behind him, Bear was working overtime with the paddle to keep the raft straight and steady. Jack looked up ahead, and blinked with surprise.

The water went *downhill*, and then *up* again. There was a dip in the water, but it stayed still. And it was right across their way.

"Bear ..." he called, and pointed.

"Got it," Bear replied. "It's called a standing wave – just two currents meeting. There'll be a bit of a bump, but we should float over it."

The raft came to the dip and shot downward. At the lowest point, the front end of the raft dug into the water and a wall of water hit Jack square in the face and chest.

But it was like when they had been running across the rocks. Jack had been prepared for it. He didn't yell, but instead he braced himself and shook the wave off.

"Great job, Jack. Keep going, buddy!"

Jack shook his head like a dog to clear the spray from his eyes. The raft shot up the other side of the dip and headed on.

After that Jack stopped worrying because he simply didn't have time. The river swept them onward, and he kept scanning the surface ahead for any obstacles.

The raft wasn't trembling anymore as it reached smoother water. It moved between the cliffs on either side as easily as if it was on wheels, faster than Jack normally walked.

After a while, the river became wider. There was a shoreline again on one side. Jack assumed Bear would head to land. They had only built the raft in the first place because they had run out of land.

But they kept going straight ahead.

"We're making great progress, Jack. You good if we keep going?" Bear said.

Jack was surprised to realize he didn't mind. The raft floated. Water came up through the gaps, but it always went away again. And a little part of him was actually enjoying the ride.

"Okay. I guess it makes sense; we won't use any energy and we're moving really well now," Jack said.

Bear smiled.

And so they kept going. The raft floated on for a long time untroubled by obstacles. It was quite peaceful, Jack thought, now that he'd gotten used to it.

Jack could see down the gorge for a couple of miles. After that, it went around a corner and he couldn't see any farther. But a few hundred feet ahead there was a thin, straight line drawn across the river. Like the water just stopped.

Jack frowned, and looked more

carefully. And listened. He could hear a new noise. Something between a hiss and a roar.

"Bear, I think there's something ahead," he said urgently.

Bear quickly began to paddle the raft toward some overhanging trees.

"Quick. Paddle left, Jack. And hard!"

"Is there danger ahead?" Jack replied

with a slight wobble to his voice.

"Rapids. Change of plan. Time to head for shore."

The raft moved sideways as they paddled, but the river still carried it forward. The line was getting nearer and the noise was getting louder. Jack felt his heart begin to pound again.

"Almost there," Bear said. Then, more urgently, "Jack, look out!"

Jack had been so busy worrying about reaching the shore that he'd stopped looking in front of him. He jerked his head around just in time to see the branch. It hung down low as it brushed across the raft and pushed him into the river.

Jack fumbled for the surface, gasping for air.

"Help!"

The roar of the water grew louder and louder, as the current swept him toward the rapids ...

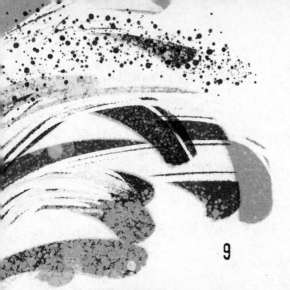

9

FLOATING WITH ATTITUDE

Jack started to thrash his arms and legs, panicking and struggling.

He just heard Bear's yell from the shore before his head went under the water again.

"Jack! Remember what I said. Float with attitude and keep your feet facing forward! I'm coming for you."

Float with attitude. That had been Bear's

first piece of advice for if he ended up in the river.

Jack immediately stopped struggling, and deliberately rolled onto his back, with his feet in front of him. He breathed in deeply. *Calm. Keep calm*, he told himself.

It was just in time!

He had reached the line in the water that was the edge of the rapids, and then just like that the current swept him over.

For a split second, Jack looked down a slope of raging white water and rocks. Then he was sliding feetfirst down a chute of water, straight at a rock surrounded by a skirt of white foam.

In the corner of his eye he saw Bear running fast along the bank.

"Aim for the side!" he shouted. "Swim to me hard now, Jack!"

Everything was a blur. But it was too late to aim anywhere. Jack's boots hit the rock and the river poured over his head. The pull of the water spun him around and carried him on past the rock. Now he was going headfirst.

Jack's shallow-end swimming really hadn't prepared him for this.

He struggled and kicked while the current swept him on, until his feet were in front again. Just in time to kick off another rock heading fast toward him.

How long had it been since he had breathed? Jack realized he must have

been holding his breath all this time. He puffed it out and took a deep gasp, just in time for a wave of water to slap him in the face.

"Gah-spthl-flg!"

Jack choked and tried to spit the water out. His body got hit by two different currents at once, which were swirling in different directions between a pair of boulders. His feet went one way and his head went another, and he spun around so fast that he totally lost his sense of direction.

Another splash of water over his head blinded him. Jack shook the water out of his eyes, just in time to see that he was

aiming headfirst for another drop.

Aim for the center! Jack remembered that.

Bear had said that if you were going over a drop, the center was the place to be. It would be deepest there.

Jack tried hard to push himself across into the main part of the flow and to get his body into the feetfirst position.

Bear was still running alongside him.

"Good job, Jack!" he shouted. "Keep focused – you can do this, buddy!"

And that was the last Jack heard as he dropped over the edge.

The water plunged six feet straight down into a frothing pool.

For half a second he was in midair. Instinctively Jack curled up into a ball and hit the pool below like a rock.

The torrent pushed Jack down into the depths. His ears pounded. All he could see was murk and bubbles pressed up against his eyeballs. Jack's lungs were bursting and he had no idea which way was up. He had a sudden fear that he was just going to go deeper and deeper and would never come up again.

Follow the bubbles and swim for the surface.

Bubbles go up, Bear had said. It's what they do. They will always head up.

Jack followed the specks swirling in front of his eyes. His head broke through the surface again and he pulled in another badly needed breath.

The waterfall was behind him. And he was still alive.

Jack could see now that he was in a long stretch of rough water. Once again he kicked until his feet were in front.

He could sort of steer by twisting his waist and moving his hands underwater like fish fins.

This was as good a chance as he would get, he told himself. It was now or never to break out and make it to the bank.

There were some rocks sticking out that would be the perfect get-out point if he could grab hold of them.

He could see Bear on the bank up ahead.

"Jack!" Bear called out. He jabbed his hands down the river. "Swim hard for the side. I'll be your backstop if you miss the get-out point."

Jack turned to the shore and swam with all his might.

Attitude and purpose, he told himself. *You can do this, Jack.*

Suddenly he realized something.

He wasn't afraid! He was surviving!

Jack was so surprised that he almost stopped swimming.

Wow! Look at me. I'm actually going to survive this!

The end was in sight. Another thirty seconds and he would be in the shallows and the calm, smooth water.

"I'm not afraid!" Jack shouted.

He could see Bear racing back up the shoreline toward him, smiling.

"I'm not afraid!"

He was up to his waist in water, now in the shallows, and he had to shake the last drops off his head and blink the water out of his eyes.

"Uh ... good?" said a slightly surprised voice.

Jack stared up in astonishment. That wasn't Bear.

He was sitting in the ditch at camp.

And Charlie, Joe and Fatima were looking down at him.

10

STUMPED

Charlie and Joe helped heave Jack out of the ditch.

"Nice fall," Charlie said cheerfully.

Jack looked down at himself. He was soaked from the waist down. From the waist up, he was bone-dry.

He took a careful look back at the ditch. The stream trickled gently along the bottom.

What?

"So, uh, since you're not afraid, maybe we should get moving?" Joe said. Without looking back, he and Charlie headed over to the cave entrance. Jack remembered that they had been heading for the control point.

Fatima hung back.

"I'm glad you didn't hurt yourself," she said.

Jack's mind was spinning. He didn't really know what to say.

"Well, uh, it wasn't far to fall," he managed to reply. "But thanks."

His sweatpants were absolutely sopping. He took fistfuls of cloth in his hands and squeezed so that water trickled out between his fingers.

"Um, could I ask you a favor?" Fatima said shyly, as Jack tried to wring his pants out. "It'll sound really silly ..."

"No, go on," Jack said. However silly her favor sounded, it couldn't be any stranger than what was going through his mind right now.

He remembered spending a day and a night beside a huge roaring river. And he remembered surviving rapids and floating down a raging river – all on his own. Well, except for his friend and guide, Bear.

But it was pretty obvious none of the others had noticed any time passing at all.

Fatima handed him her orienteering sheet.

"Could you get this stamped in there?" She nodded at the cave.

There was something in the way she

was looking at him that Jack recognized. Her mouth was clamped a little too tight. There was a very faint hint of a tremble by her lips.

He knew those signs.

It was like when he didn't want anyone to know he was scared.

Jack wondered what she was frightened of. Bats? Spiders? It could be anything you might find in a cave. He didn't want to embarrass her by asking.

Maybe one day she would meet someone like Bear, who could help with whatever it was. He looked at the strain on her face and remembered how kind and encouraging Bear had been.

"Sure," he said, taking the sheet.

The cave wasn't big. The stamp was a plastic widget tied to a picnic table at the end, so no one could take it. Jack stamped his and Fatima's sheets, and carried them back outside to join the others.

"Thanks so much," she said, putting the sheet in her map wallet. "I got split up from my team and I think they've already gone ahead."

"Why don't you finish the course with us, then?" Jack said with a smile, and she smiled back.

"Thank you!"

The last control point was by the lake. The four friends jogged along the beach toward it.

"Last one there has to smell Charlie's T-shirt!" Joe yelled, and broke into a run.

"Hey!" Charlie shouted indignantly, and he pelted after Joe. Fatima and Jack laughed, and then Fatima stumbled.

"Oh, hang on. My lace is undone."

Her map wallet rustled in the breeze as she put it down on the ground. Just as she pulled her laces tight, a gust of wind

blew the wallet into the air and it got caught in some branches that stuck out over the lake.

"Oh, I don't believe it!" Fatima groaned.

Jack and Fatima stood on the shore looking up.

"It's not far," Jack said thoughtfully. "If I stand on that branch there, I can reach it."

"No," Fatima said with resignation, "let me. You could fall in."

Jack patted his sweatpants and laughed. "Hey, I'm already soaked!"

He gave her his own wallet to hold. Then he hoisted himself up onto the lower branch, and carefully pulled himself up to his feet. Jack held on to the higher-up branch, and sidled out across the water.

The branch he was standing on began to bend under his weight.

Jack kept working his way along. The plastic wallet was getting closer …

But then Jack realized it was also getting farther away, as the branch bent down toward the water. Even though he stretched up as high as he could, his fingers couldn't quite reach the wallet.

"Don't worry, Jack," Fatima called. "It's not worth it."

"Hey, I've come this far!" Jack replied. There was still one way to do this.

He flexed his knees, and jumped with his arms held up. His fingers snatched at the wallet and held on, just as he started to come down again.

Jack grinned as he hit the water backward.

"*Woot!*" he yelled happily as he stood up. Water poured off him in every direction.

"You're crazy!" Fatima laughed as he waded back to shore. Jack laughed too as he handed her the waterproof wallet.

"I guess I'd better go and get changed."

"I hope you didn't lose anything in the lake."

"Nah, I just had the compass on me and ..." As Jack pulled the compass out of his pocket to show her he realized there was something else in there. What was that?

Jack's voice trailed off as he saw what he had just pulled from his pocket.

It was a stump of bamboo.

With tooth marks on it.

His panda souvenir!

"Um – why have you got a bit of chewed-up bamboo in your pocket?" Fatima asked.

"Good question ..."

Jack murmured as he stared at it.

Then he remembered that moment at the cave. Fatima had been scared of … something. He still didn't know what.

But he did know someone who could help. He had the bamboo – his adventure had been real.

Had the compass guided him to Bear? Could it do the same for her?

Stage one: believe.

Jack held the compass out. "Here, this is for you. It's a gift."

And with that, Jack ran off to join his teammates.

The End

Bear Grylls got the taste for adventure at a young age from his father, a former Royal Marine. After school, Bear joined the Reserve SAS, then went on to become one of the youngest people ever to climb Mount Everest, just two years after breaking his back in three places during a parachute jump.

Among other adventures he has led expeditions to the Arctic and the Antarctic, crossed oceans and set world records in skydiving and paragliding.

Bear is also a bestselling author and the host of television programs such as *Survival School* and *The Island*.

He has shared his survival skills with people all over the world, and has taken many famous movie stars and sports stars on adventures – and even President Barack Obama!

Bear Grylls is Chief Scout to the UK Scouting Association, encouraging young people to have great adventures, follow their dreams and to look after their friends. Bear is also honorary Colonel to the Royal Marine Commandos.

When Bear's not traveling the world, he lives with his wife and three sons on a barge in London, or on an island off the coast of Wales.

Find out more at **www.beargrylls.com**

READ THEM ALL